WALLY MEETS
DINA DINOSAUR

Written by Carolyn Webster-Stratton, Ph.D.

Wally is seven years old and he goes to elementary school. He is very strong and smart about many things. For example, he knows how to put together extremely complicated models. He also knows all about many different kinds of dinosaurs. He knows what they weigh, how tall they are, what they eat and even what they are called. But Wally feels different from the other kids at school.

Everyone else at school seems to be able to sit still for a very long time. But no matter how hard Wally tries he just can't be still. He feels wiggly and squirmy inside. Sometimes he blurts out the answer in class without raising his hand. Sometimes he needs to move so badly that he pretends he needs to sharpen his pencil or go to the bathroom so he can get up from his desk. Sometimes his hands twitch and tap, his legs wiggle, and he makes noises under his breath and he doesn't even know he is doing this until his teacher yells at him to stop!

Sometimes he works so hard to stay still in the classroom that when he gets out for recess, he seems to explode. He runs around wildly, often disrupting the other kids' play. His classmates either get mad at him or tease and laugh at him. They don't let him play with them because they say he is too wild and crazy.

But Wally has another problem that he is even more afraid to talk about. He can't read! He is convinced that all the other kids can read. So he pretends to read at reading time but he just can't make out most of the words. It looks like a foreign language to him.

He thinks his teacher and his parents are disappointed and angry with him. They often yell at him and tell him to concentrate and listen more. He always seems to get punished for something, even when he hasn't done anything! One day he heard his teacher tell his mother that he was like a wild animal in class and needed a tranquilizer. Wally felt very lonely.

Wally began to think that he was really an alien in disguise from another planet. He thought maybe he was a kind of alien dinosaur. He began to imagine that he was with other alien dinosaurs who were just like him and loved to run and explore wild places. They would hang out together in groups speaking their own special language.

One day when he was sitting at his desk daydreaming about being an alien he suddenly found himself looking at a green and blue, polka-dotted dinosaur.

"Hi Wally," said Dina. "I'm Dina, the last living dinosaur on earth. I'm one hundred million years old."

"Cool," said Wally trying to figure what kind of dinosaur she was. Her duckbilled mouth made her look like a Prosaurologphus but her fingers and thumb indicated she might be an Iguanodon. At least thought Wally, both of these are herbivores so I'm probably not in danger. But her wings didn't fit any kind of dinosaur Wally knew anything about!

"How did you survive so long on earth when none of the other dinosaurs did?" asked Wally.

"Oh, I nearly didn't survive," said Dina. "You see there were all these survival rules we dinosaurs were supposed to follow. You know like not fighting with the carnivorous dinosaurs and not flying too near the volcanos and listening to your parents about what to eat or not to eat and swiftly following their directions and not straying from the herd when traveling. Well I could see that the dinosaurs who didn't follow the rules were quickly becoming extinct! So I made up my own personal list of Dinosaur Survival Rules."

"Wow," said Wally, "I thought dinosaurs became extinct because of a meteorite striking the earth causing big changes in the climate."

"Oh no," said Dina, "we could have survived that if we had followed the survival rules."

"Would you tell me what those rules are?" asked Wally.

"I will," said Dina, "but only if you promise to share them with other alien Dinosaurs," and Wally agreed.

"Okay," said Wally.

Rules

DINOSAUR RULE 1: Exercise your mind and your body.

Exercise your body whenever you can but remember to fly around only in safe places.

Exercise your mind too. Not only does your body need exercise but your mind does too.

Remember when you feel like you have to run but know you have to keep quiet because there is a dangerous animal near by, try tightening your body one muscle at a time, and then letting it go limp.

DINOSAUR RULE 2: Listen, think and solve problems.

Listen to parent and teacher Dinosaurs. They can help keep you out of trouble.

When you have a problem, try to think of as many different solutions as you can, and when one solution doesn't work try another one.

When you're angry, try to calm down by taking some deep breaths. Or try pretending your mind has a special screen and you can show relaxing pictures there. For example, imagine a happy place where you are feeling calm. Once you are calm, think up safe and fair ways to solve problems.

DINOSAUR RULE 3: Have courage.

Have the courage to admit you're scared and ask for someone else's help.

Sharing your feelings of being scared with someone you trust can help you feel less lonely.

DINOSAUR RULE 4: Be friendly.

Pay a friend a compliment.

Being a friend means lots of sharing. Remember your friend doesn't have to be a dinosaur. Friends like each other just the way they are.

DINOSAUR RULE 5: Believe in yourself.

Remember all dinosaurs are different. Don't worry about what you can't do, think about what you can do.

Remember all Dinosaurs make mistakes!

Face up to what is upsetting you; sometimes your imagination is worse than in reality.